"You bet!" he says and he springs high into the air.

Top-Hat Fox is watching from behind the tent.

"Hmmmm," he says to himself, "he's going to be perfect for my circus."

Everyone rushes into the big tent.

"Welcome to my circus!" announces Top-Hat Fox. "You will see incredible feats!"

"Behold the Flying Bearlendas!" says Top-Hat Fox. "They are the best trapeze artists in the world!"

"Yay!" shouts the Cat family.
They sit in the very first row.
"I can't wait to see Lowly Worm," says Sally.
"Me either," says Huckle.

Meanwhile, Top-Hat Fox has given Lowly Worm a costume and is showing him around the circus.

"This is Miss Puss," says Top-Hat Fox. "She can bend into *any* shape."

Soon it is show time! Lowly takes a deep breath.

"Here I come!" he says, and he hops into the big tent.

Top-Hat Fox bows to the audience.

"And now," he announces, "performing for the first time. The one . . . the only . . . Lowly Worm!"

Lowly amazes the crowd by juggling four bowling pins.

Then he tosses them up . . .

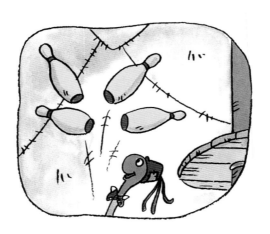

and catches them in midair!

"Oooh!" shouts the crowd. "He's amazing."

When the show is over, everyone crowds around Lowly.

"Lowly, Lowly!" they scream.

"Can I have your autograph?"

"Me too?"

After the audience has left, the circus performers start to pack up.

"You were terrific, Lowly," says Top-Hat Fox. "We'll be in Pleasantville tomorrow."

Lowly gulps. "But how will I get home to my family?" he asks.

"We're your new family, Lowly," says Top-Hat Fox. "And the circus is your new home."

Lowly feels terrible. He looks at a picture of Huckle, Sally, and Mother and Father Cat.

"I don't want a new family or a new home!" he says.

The Cat family is upset too.

Mother Cat stares at Lowly's empty chair.

"I sure miss Lowly," says Huckle.

"He's a circus performer now," says Father Cat sadly.

Suddenly, Lowly hops through the kitchen window!